THIS BOOK BELONGS TO:

....

....

Made in United States
Orlando, FL
06 December 2024

55093044R10055